Our special dedication is to all our grandchildren whose love of reading and being read to have inspired all of us to want to write the new tales of the Irish Leprechaun.

Anna Kelly
Isabella O'Brien
Sofia O'Brien
Daniel O'Brien
Julie Stapleton
Benjamin Gravine
Jack Gravine
Noah Gravine

www.mascotbooks.com

The Next Notre Dame Mascot

For more information, please contact:
Mascot Books
560 Herndon Parkway #120
Herndon, VA 20170
info@mascotbooks.com

CPSIA Code: PRT0615A
ISBN-13: 978-1-63177-056-2

Printed in the United States

The Next NOTRE DAME® Mascot

Written by **The Four Pops**

Illustrated by **Adam Schartup**

On a crisp, fall day, Mascot Mike led the Notre Dame Football team onto the field. It was a special day for Mike; he was celebrating his twelfth birthday. In human years, he was eighty-four years old! Mike couldn't jump as high as he used to, and he was always sleepy. Sometimes, he was caught snoring after the halftime show!

After the football game, Mike thought about his younger days. When the Notre Dame Football team scored a touchdown, Mike would do six forward flips. For extra points, he would do backward flips. Then, with the school flag in his mouth, Mike would run up and down the sidelines. The fans would all cheer! *Hooray!* But Mike knew it was time to find a new mascot.

When Mike met with Regis, the team's manager, they agreed that it was time for Mike to retire. *He gave so much for the team, who could replace him?* thought Regis. *Who will be the next mascot? Can we find another Irish terrier?*

Regis placed an ad for a new mascot in the local newspaper, the *South Bend Tribune.*

The cheerleaders volunteered to be the judges in picking the new mascot and made a poster with the qualifications.

When the day for tryouts arrived, characters of all kinds showed up to impress.

Contestant after contestant, the cheerleaders just couldn't find the right fit. The chipmunk knew his Notre Dame trivia, but he couldn't do a flip. The superhero could do hundreds of pushups, but he didn't even know when Notre Dame was founded!

It all came down to the Irish jig…

Never before had the cheerleaders seen so many funny versions of the Irish jig. Contestant after contestant flailed about, and each fall had everyone laughing. After all the laughing, the cheerleaders noticed that one contestant was not only still on his feet, but dancing quite well.

The cheerleaders huddled together discussing the results.

"He did front *and* back flips!" one cheerleader said.

"He knows more Notre Dame Trivia than I do!"
said another.

After a lengthy discussion, the cheerleaders
turned to the mascots and announced, "The new Notre
Dame mascot is…the Leprechaun!"

The Leprechaun was so excited, he did front flips
all the way to the end of the gym.

On his first game day, the Leprechaun practiced somersaults and pushups in the locker room, with Mike there to guide him. Just before game time, the Leprechaun peeked into the stadium. When he saw the large crowd, the Leprechaun backed away from the door, timidly sat down on the floor, and pulled his hat down over his head.

"What's the matter?" asked Mike.

"I've never seen so many people before! I don't think I can make that many people cheer."

"Don't worry, I was nervous my first time, too. You just have to get up, go out there, and cheer your heart out!"

On a beautiful fall afternoon, Mike set out for his last day of glory. He and the Leprechaun ran onto the football field together, ready to start the cheers. Mike barked as loud as he could to get the crowd's attention. Together, Mike and the Leprechaun did a forward flip, then a backward flip, and bowed.

The crowd jumped out of their seats and cheered!

Over the loud speaker, the announcer said, "Thank you, Mike, for your years of being our mascot. We all love you!"

"Now, let's welcome our new mascot, the Leprechaun!"

The Leprechaun led the Notre Dame Football team onto the field.

Goooo Irish!

About the Authors

The Four Pops are Glenn Davis, Daniel O'Brien, Mark Smith, and Tom Stapleton. All are former teachers enjoying their retirement, spending time with their grandchildren, playing shuffle board, watching Monday Night Football together, and going to Notre Dame football games.

About Mascot Mike

Irish Terriers have been part of the Notre Dame football history as a mascot since the early 1900s. In the 1960s, the Leprechaun joined the ranks of the cheerleaders on the sidelines. By the end of the decade, the terriers had slowly faded into history.

Log into our website www.FourPops.com to find out more about the authors, the book, and our future projects.